A Note to Parents

Read to your child...

★ Reading aloud is one of the best ways to develop your child's love of reading. Read together at least 20 minutes each day.

★ Laughter is contagious! Read with feeling. Show your child that reading is fun.

★ Take time to answer questions your child may have about the story. Linger over pages that interest your child.

...and your child will read to you.

★ Follow cues from your child to know when he wants to join in the reading.

★ Support your young reader. Give him a word whenever he asks for it.

★ Praise your child as he progresses. Your encouraging words will build his confidence.

You can help your Level 1 reader.

★ Reading begins with knowing how a book works. Show your child the title and where the story begins.

★ Ask your child to find picture clues on each page. Talk about what is happening in the story.

★ Point to the words as you read so your child can make the connection between the print and the story.

★ Ask your child to point to words she knows.

★ Let your child supply the rhyming words.

Most of all, enjoy your reading time together!

Library of Congress Cataloging-in-Publication Data

Goldowsky, Jill.
    Lost and found puppy / by Jill Goldowsky ; illustrated by Jennifer Fitchwell.
        p. cm — (All-star readers. Level 1)
    Summary: A brother and sister enjoy playing with their new pet puppy, but then they
discover that he is missing.
    ISBN 0-7944-0383-2
    [1. Dogs—Fiction. 2. Lost and found possessions—Fiction 3. Brothers and
sisters—Fiction] I. Fitchwell, Jennifer, ill. II. Title. III. Series.

PZ7.G5696Lo 2004
[E]—dc21
                                                                2003046803

Lost and Found Puppy

by Jill L. Goldowsky
illustrated by Jennifer Fitchwell

All-Star Readers®

Reader's Digest Children's Books™
Pleasantville, New York • Montréal, Québec

Mom came home with a big surprise.

Dad told us
to close our eyes.

It's a new pup!
His name is Jack.

His fur is brown.
His nose is black.

We scratched his ears.

He licked our faces.

He likes to play
and chew our laces.

At the park,
Jack played ball.

We gave Jack a bath.

He splashed us all!

Then one day there was no Jack.

We called his name.
Jack didn't come back!

We went to the park
and called Jack's name.

We shouted, "Jack! Jack!"
but Jack never came.

We went to town
to hang signs up.

Lost Puppy
Jack

Had anyone seen our little lost pup?

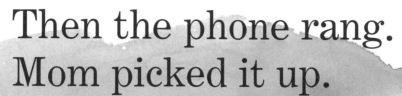

Then the phone rang.
Mom picked it up.

A person asked,
"Have you lost a pup?"

His fur is brown.
His nose is black."

Now Jack is home.
He licks our faces.

He likes to play
and chew our laces.

Color in the star next to each word you can read.

☆ a
☆ all
☆ and
☆ anyone
☆ asked
☆ at
☆ back
☆ ball
☆ bath
☆ big
☆ black
☆ brown
☆ but
☆ called
☆ came
☆ chew
☆ close
☆ come
☆ Dad
☆ day
☆ didn't

☆ ears
☆ eyes
☆ faces
☆ fur
☆ gave
☆ had
☆ hang
☆ have
☆ he
☆ his
☆ home
☆ is
☆ it
☆ it's
☆ Jack
☆ laces
☆ little
☆ licked
☆ licks
☆ likes
☆ lost

☆ Mom
☆ name
☆ never
☆ new
☆ no
☆ nose
☆ now
☆ one
☆ our
☆ park
☆ person
☆ phone
☆ picked
☆ play
☆ played
☆ pup
☆ rang
☆ said
☆ scratched
☆ seen
☆ shouted

☆ signs
☆ splashed
☆ surprise
☆ the
☆ there
☆ then
☆ to
☆ told
☆ town
☆ up
☆ us
☆ was
☆ we
☆ welcome
☆ went
☆ with
☆ yes
☆ you